To Tamir Rice,
Trayvon Martin,
EJ Bradford,
Jordan Edwards,
Michael Brown,
Jordan Davis,
and Julian Mallory.

– D.B.

To my son, Gabriel,
and all little brothers like him.

– G.C.J.

First published in the US in 2020 by Nancy Paulsen Books,
an imprint of Penguin Random House LLC, New York
First published in Great Britain in 2020 by Farshore

An imprint of HarperCollins*Publishers*
1 London Bridge Street
London SE1 9GF
www.farshore.co.uk

Text copyright © Derrick Barnes 2020
Illustrations copyright © Gordon C. James 2020

The moral rights of Derrick Barnes and Gordon C. James have been asserted.

ISBN 978 0 7555 0270 7
002
Printed in the UK by Pureprint a CarbonNeutral® company.

MIX
Paper from
responsible sources
FSC
www.fsc.org   FSC™ C007454

This book is produced from independently certified FSC™ paper
to ensure responsible forest management.

For more information visit: www.harpercollins.co.uk/green

I AM EVERY GOOD THING

DERRICK BARNES

illustrated by

GORDON C. JAMES

I am a non-stop ball of energy.
Powerful and full of light.
I am a go-getter. A difference-maker.
A leader.

I am every good thing that makes the world go round.
You know – like gravity, or the glow of moonbeams
over a field of brand-new snow.

I am good to the core, like the centre
of a cinnamon roll.

Yeah, that good.

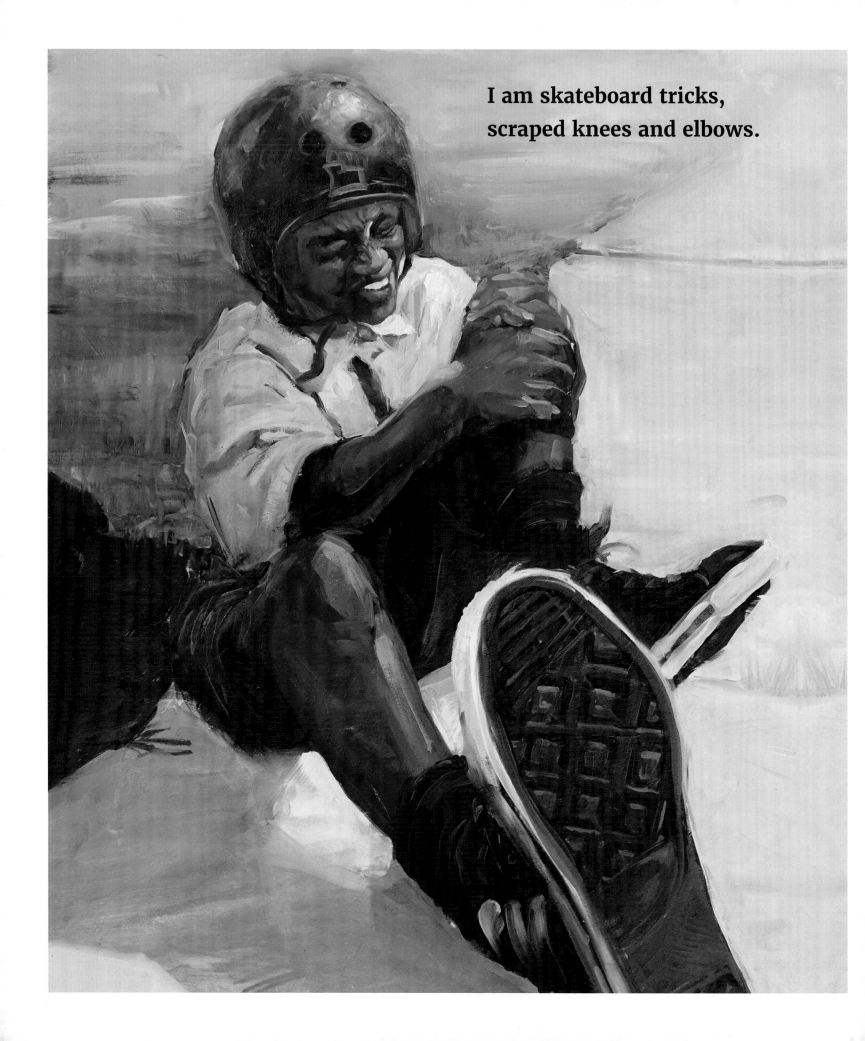

I am skateboard tricks,
scraped knees and elbows.

But you know what?
I am right back on
my feet again.

I am one eye open, one eye closed,
peeking through a microscope,
gazing through a telescope,
checking out the spaces around me
and plotting out those far-off places
I have yet to go – but will.

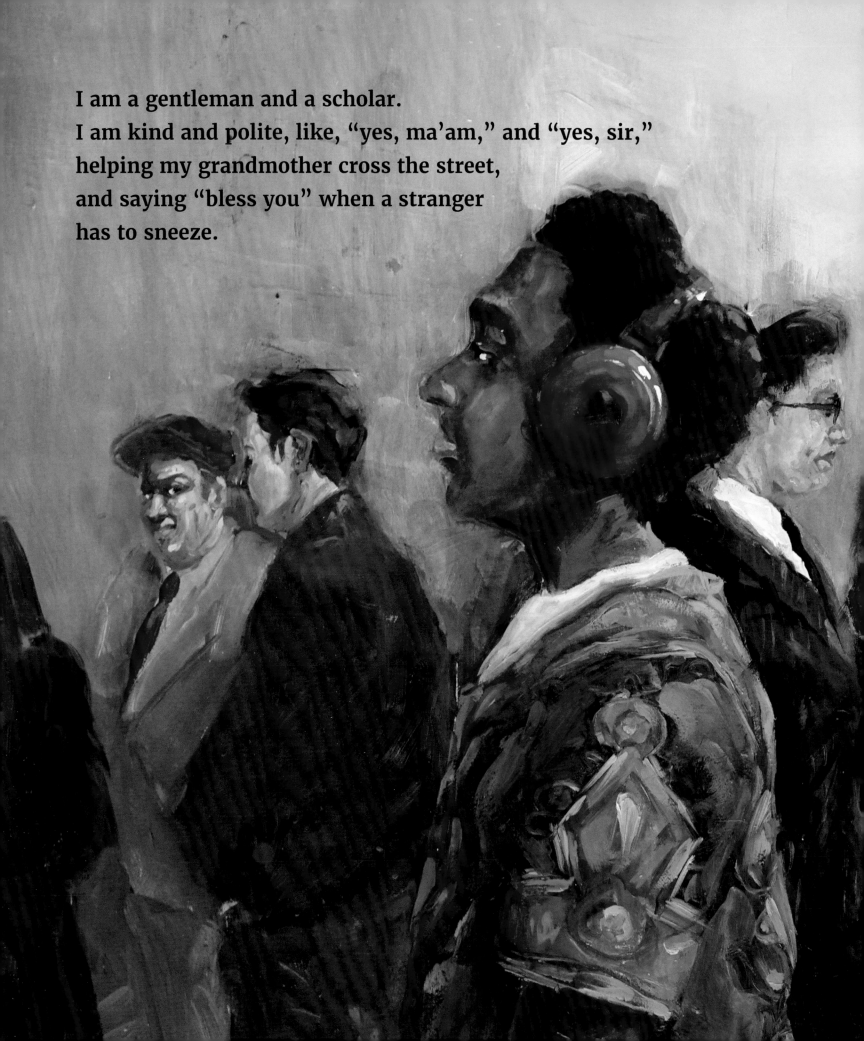

I am a gentleman and a scholar.
I am kind and polite, like, "yes, ma'am," and "yes, sir,"
helping my grandmother cross the street,
and saying "bless you" when a stranger
has to sneeze.

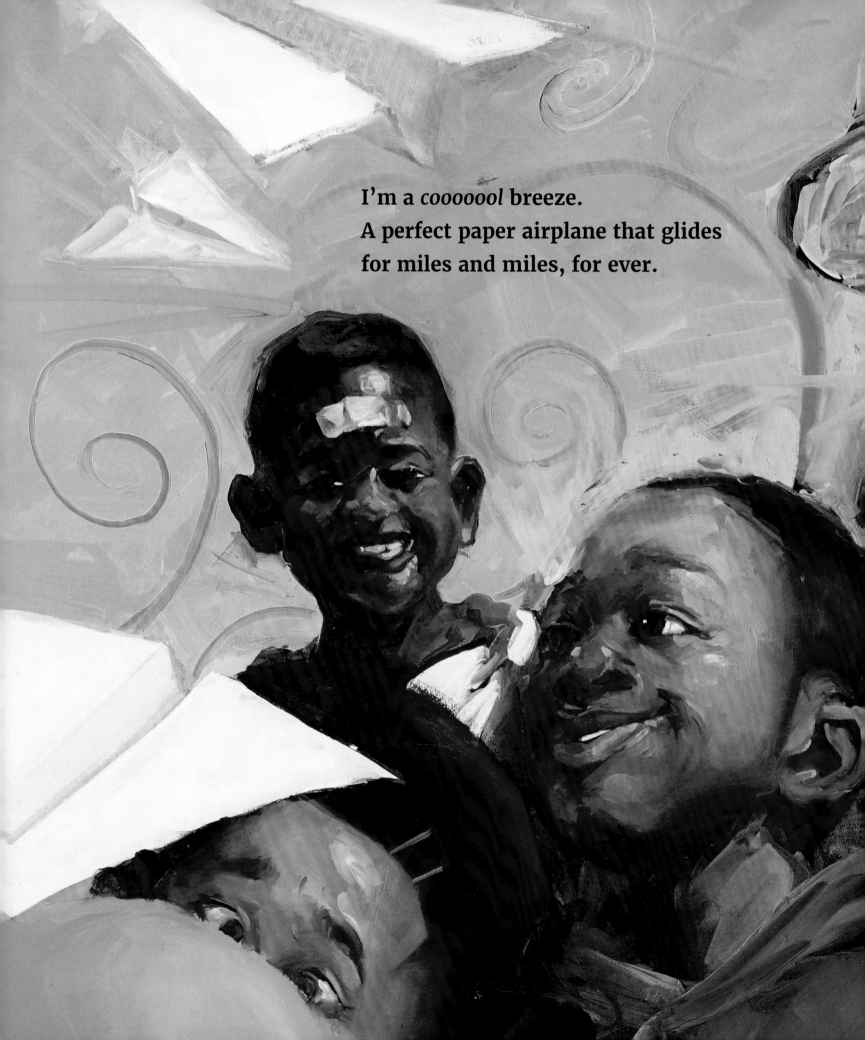

I'm a *coooooool* breeze.
A perfect paper airplane that glides
for miles and miles, for ever.

I am a roaring flame of creativity.
I am a lightning round of questions and
a star-filled sky of solutions.
I am an explorer, planting a flag on every
bit of this planet where I belong.
I am a sponge, soaking up information,
knowledge and wisdom.
I want it all, and I am *allllll* ears.

I am Saturday mornings in the summertime.
I am two bounces and a front flip
off the diving board.
I am hilarious. I am the life of the party.
I am that smile forming on your face right now.

I am a brother,
a son,
a nephew,
a favourite cousin,
a grandson.
I am a friend.
I am real.

I am tight hugs, a hand
to hold, a shoulder to cry
on – if you have to.
I hope you never have to.
I am here.

I'm the *BOOM-BAP –*
BOOM-BOOM-BAP
when the bass line thumps and the
kick drum jumps.
I'm the perfect beat, the perfect rhyme,
keeping everything on point and
always on time –
but you already knew that.

Although I am something like a superhero,
every now and then,
I am afraid.

I am not what they might call me,
and I will not answer to any name
that is not my own.
I am what I say I am.

I am brave. I am hope.
I am my ancestors' wildest dream.

I am worthy of success, of respect, of safety,
of kindness, of happiness.

And without a shadow
of a doubt,
I am worthy
to be loved.

**I am worthy
to be loved.**